This book belongs to

Please read it to me.
Thank you!

Pickles
and the Party

Written by Joan K. Moore
Illustrated by Arjaa Raghu

Published by Idea Storm Press
Lake Zurich, Illinois

IBSN 978-0-9820686-8-7

www.jkmhappy.com

Dedication:

To my Mama who taught me,
"Nobody is better than you and
you are no better than anybody."

Characters...

Pickles

Daughter of Tiny & Mr. Sims

Fancy

Pickles' Friend

Tiny

Pickles' Mother

Mr. Sims

Pickles' Father

Bodine

Pickles' Brother

Lucy

Pickles' Friend

Miss Smith

Pickles' Teacher

Mama Belle lives in a big farmhouse
in Kettle, Kentucky. Her friendly cats, Mr. Sims
and Tiny, and their kittens, Pickles and Bodine,
live in the barn on the farm.

Pickles is kind and friendly to everyone.

One day, it surprised her to learn that not everyone
wanted to be *her* friend.

In the school lunchroom, Pickles overheard some
kittens talking about Fancy's birthday party.   There
was just one problem…
Pickles had not been invited.

Pickles wanted to go to Fancy's party. Who would not want to go? Fancy is a soft white kitten with the prettiest blue eyes and she lives with her parents in the biggest house in Kettle, Kentucky.

Pickles' friend Lucy asked,

"Are you going to Fancy's party on Saturday?"

"No, she is not coming to *my* party," Fancy interrupted. "Pickles is a *barn* cat. *Barn* cats do not know how to act in a house and I will not have her ruin *my* party."

Pickles ran from the lunchroom crying.

After school, Pickles' older brother Bodine tried to

cheer her up,

"Pickles, you would have no fun at a house party.

There are no good games to play and cats that live

in houses eat weird food."

Pickles had never felt so sad. What was wrong with her? Why was being a barn cat so bad?

It did not take long for her parents to learn what
happened. By now, Pickles was not just hurt,
she was angry.

"I will show Fancy!" Pickles hissed.

"Who does she think she is, calling me names?

She is nothing but a prissy little ball of white fluff

who cannot even add double digits. Living in that

big house does not make her special.

It makes her dumb and lazy!"

Pickles started to say more when her mother stopped her.

"Pickles," Tiny said sternly, "you need to stop talking like that right now!"

"Your mother is right," said Mr. Sims.

"When someone hurts you,

it is not right to hurt them back."

"But," Pickles said, "Fancy made fun of me because

of where I live. She said I was not

good enough to come to her party.

I will show her who is good enough."

"You will do no such thing," Tiny interrupted. "You must treat everyone with kindness and respect, even when you do not feel like it."

Tiny knew she must teach Pickles an important lesson. Tiny needed Pickles to understand that where you live, what you look like, the kind of food you eat, or even how well you can add does not make you better or worse than anyone else. It is who you are on the inside that matters.

Tiny said, "Pickles, everyone is special in his or her own way. Nobody is better than you and you are no better than anybody."

Tiny continued, "Others may still try to make you feel bad about who you are."

Pickles asked, "Why would someone do that?"

Tiny replied, "It is usually because of jealousy or fear."

"Fancy should not be jealous or afraid of me," Pickles said. "So why did she act like that?"

"That is hard to say, dear," Tiny said. "But, being a barn cat does not make you better or worse than Fancy. It just means you live in a different kind of house. You should not be unkind to Fancy."

"Okay Mama," said Pickles.

Pickles could not imagine living anywhere better
than Mama Belle's farm with her family.

The next day at school, the kittens' teacher, Miss Smith, had them adding and subtracting double digits.

Fancy struggled with the numbers. So, Miss Smith asked for a volunteer to help her.

Pickles immediately volunteered! Her kindness surprised Fancy. Pickles explained the math to her classmate in simple terms. Fancy soon discovered that math was not so hard and she could add and subtract double digits!

Fancy asked Pickles, "Why did you help me?"

Pickles explained, "I have always been nice to you Fancy. How well I can add or subtract does not make me better or worse than you. It is what is on the inside that matters."

Pickles added, "As Mama says...Nobody is better than you and you are no better than anybody."

MATH

$$25 \atop +17$$

$$22 \atop -15$$

Written by
Joan K. Moore

Joan grew up in Kettle, Kentucky, and now lives in Schaumburg, Illinois. She is the aunt of two terrific nephews, four fabulous nieces, and one great-niece.

Joan's mother taught her simple truths and valuable life lessons, which inspired her to begin writing children's books. Pickles was one of the numerous cats owned by her mother.

Illustrated by
Arjaa Raghu

Arjaa is a 10-year old,
5th grader who attends
Owen Elementary School.

She lives in Aurora, Illinois, with her parents Mythreye and
Raghu, grandma Padmasini, and brother Adithya.

Arjaa enjoys dancing, singing, drawing, and playing video
games. She enjoyed illustrating *Pickles and the Party*.

art studio for children and adults

Studio nafisa believes that study of art develops an open and creative mind that has long lasting impact on an individual's ability to innovate and be successful.

The studio offers:
- classes for drawing, sketching, painting, crafts, mixed media art
- art parties for birthdays and other celebrations
- camps for kids during school breaks
- open studio hours and facility for amateur and experienced artists
- group events for art badge, patch, belt loop, pin requirements for Girl Scouts, Cub Scouts and Boy Scouts
- art enrichment and after school program

Arjaa, the illustrator of this book, is a student of studio nafisa.
She received special coaching at the studio to illustrate the book.

studio nafisa
Website : www.studionafisa.com
Facebook: www.facebook.com/studionafisa
Address: 4260 Westbrook Drive, #101, Aurora, IL 60504

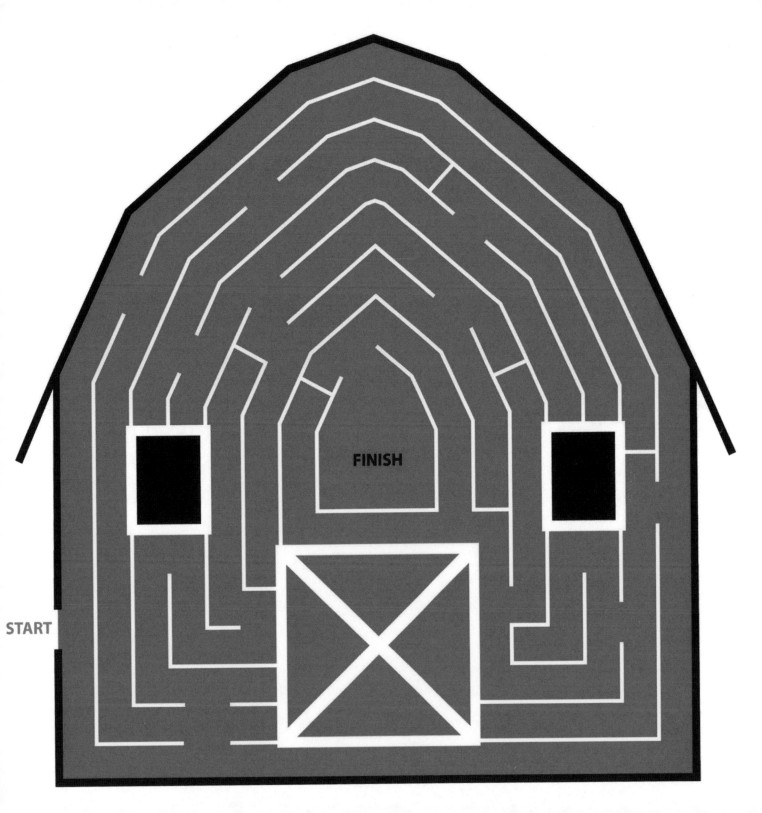

START

FINISH

Also available...
P-i-c-k-l-e-s Spells Pickles

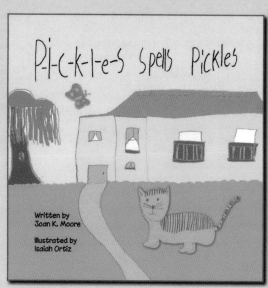

P-i-c-k-l-e-s Spells Pickles

Written by
Joan K. Moore

Illustrated by
Isaiah Ortiz

available at amazon.com

Coming soon ...

Pickles
Tells the Truth

Made in the USA
Lexington, KY
28 January 2016